Pun Mastery

Agile Jokes For Agile Folks

by
Nigel Baker, Paul Goddard &
Geoff Watts

Illustrated by Stuart Young

To Andrew

Cover Design by Nigel Baker
Illustrations by Stuart Young

First Edition Published 2021 by Inspect & Adapt Ltd
96 Redgrove Park, Cheltenham, Glos, GL51 6QZ

Introduction

We came up with this because we were bored during lockdown.

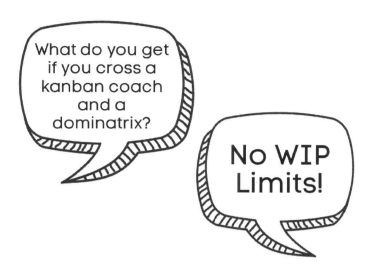

I saw two chickens pecking away at a laptop the other day.

They must have been Eggs-treme programmers.

What do you call a business partner who has no stakeholders?

A Product Loner!

A developer, a ScrumMaster and an agile coach walk into a bar.

The developer buys a drink.

The ScrumMaster sets up a retrospective around the drink-buying process.

The agile coach charges £1,000 to facilitate it.

From the agile lie-brary...

DID YOU HEAR THAT,
BRUCE SPRINGSTEEN'S
E-STREET BAND IS
STARTING TO USE SCRUM?

THEY ARE BECOMING
BOSS-FUNCTIONAL!

Why did the agile coach cross the road?

Because she was a chicken not a pig.

Why did the Product Owner turn back while crossing the road?

Because a Product Owner ALWAYS changes their mind!

Why did the stupid ScrumMaster come to work dressed as Elvis?

Because he thought he was attending a retro-spective.

There once was an eager ScrumMaster,
Who wanted his team to go faster,
He strapped on a rocket,
He found in his pocket,
They were last seen high over Nebraska!

I just did a training course on how to clean my dirty patio with a jet wash.

I'm now a Certified Scum-Blaster.

Bottleneck (*noun*)

(1) The part of the process where production tends to slow down as it doesn't have the capacity to process as much work as the rest of the process. A prime opportunity for increasing throughput and flow therefore productivity;

(2) The slowest or least productive member of the team;

(3) Management.

OUR PRODUCT OWNER
WANTED US TO INCREASE
OUR VELOCITY.

SO I STOLE HIS PORSCHE!

What do you call an annoyingly loud business partner?

A Product Moaner.

Three agile coaches walk into the bar.

The developers jump out the window!

An old agile coach called Felicity,
Who had no agile authenticity,
She was massively dumb,
Knew nothing 'bout Scrum,
The completely wrong type of simplicity.

What's the difference between an agile coach and an Italian chef?

One works with a manifesto; the other works with many pestos.

How many agile coaches does it take to change a lightbulb?

Well...does the lightbulb actually want to be changed?

Why did the stupid ScrumMaster throw away their exercise bike?

She was told to reduce cycle time!

I just did a training course on how to prolong my excessive bread usage.

I'm now a Certified Crumb-Laster.

How many lean
consultants does it take to
change a lightbulb?

Two.

One to change it and the other to
tell everyone the Japanese word
for lightbulb.

My boss told me to go on an agile training course, so I looked it up on Wikipedia.

It said "Maximise the amount of work not done."

So I didn't turn up.

What's the difference between Godzilla and Jira?

One is a gigantic monstrosity that destroys everything in its path.

And the other is a big lizard.

Fun Fact: Jira is named after Gojira - the Japanese name for Godzilla.

Did you hear about the dyslexic coach who wanted to increase flow?

The team now consists of 3 chickens, 2 ducks and a particularly aggressive goose.

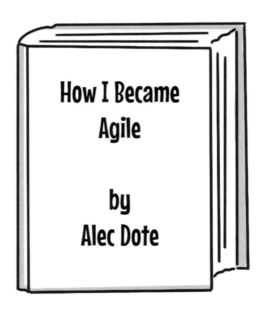

How I Became Agile

by Alec Dote

There once was a girl called Justine,
Who applied to join a scrum team.
Devouring all books in sight,
She grew in both weight and height,
Then was fired for not being lean.

Loser Story (*noun*)

(1) A user story that is never going to have a happy ending;

(2) A user story the team have to deliver for a user they have little empathy for.

Why do vampires make bad Product Owners?

Because they are terrified of stakeholders.

There was an argument between the colourists and the podiatrists at the nail salon.

They resolved it by having a red-toe-spective.

Did you hear about the agile coach crushed by his home-made information radiator?

He was *board* to death!

What's a kanban coach's favourite band?

The Kaizen Chiefs.

Inept and Accept (*phrase*)

Compared to the agile principle of inspect and adapt; the process of building something quick and dirty and then moving on, pretending you're agile.

HOW MANY PRODUCT OWNERS DOES IT TAKE TO CHANGE A LIGHTBULB?

TWO.

ONE TO CHANGE THE LIGHTBULB AND ONE TO ASK WHY IT ISN'T BRIGHT ENOUGH.

How does a Product Owner see the product backlog?

With their priorit-eyes.

I just did a training course on how to protect rectal injuries.

I'm now a Certified Bum-Plaster.

Parking Lot (*noun*)

The place where people's opinions, questions or requests go to die as they will never be picked up on again. But at least we can carry on with the meeting.

And keep to the time box.

Why did the stupid Product Owner get no guests at their wedding?

Because they didn't put acceptance criteria on the invites.

Alcoholic Estimation (*verb*)

(1) The practice of estimating product backlog items based on the number of alcoholic units a developer would require in order to tackle it.

(2) The practice of estimating a product backlog while under the influence of a significant amount of alcohol - ironically often resulting in significantly higher accuracy.

What's the most common user story?

"Give me my features or I'll make your life hell."

I just did a training course on how to ruin spirits.

I'm now a Certified Rum-Disaster.

What's the difference between a
product owner and a drugs dealer?

One horribly abuses their users
and the other sells drugs.

I saw a man sat coding in a dried up riverbed the other day.

He was trying to do Ex-Stream Programming!

Technical Bankruptcy (*phrase*)

The situation whereby so much technical debt has been accumulated that nobody has any idea how to add new functionality to what has been built, the system is so unstable that nobody wants to touch it and people are busy building a business case for a re-architecture project to replace the legacy system.

Why didn't the stupid
Product Owner get served in
the restaurant?

**Because she prioritised
instead of ordered.**

Anchoring
Estimations

by
Hugo First

What's the difference between an agile coach and Greta Thunberg?

One wants to kanban, the other wants to ban cans.

An extreme XP coach called Glenn,
Thought himself one of agile's wise men.
Even when networking,
He would carry a gherkin,
And would only say given, when, then.

Why did the stupid
Scrum Master buy a plunger?

He wanted to clear the backlog.

Daily Sit Down (*event*)

Daily meeting performed by a team, usually on Zoom, and often on the toilet. Ideally with the camera and microphone switched off.

Refactoring:

When the first hard factoring wasn't enough.

Kronenbourg (*noun*)

A story that looks initially like a 16-pointer but turns out to be more like a 64, named after the popular headache-inducing French lager "Kronenbourg 1664".

What's the difference between a Product Owner and someone desperate for the toilet?

One has a backlog; the other lacks a bog.

Why did the stupid ScrumMaster
parcel up their watches and clocks?

Because they thought Scrum was
all about timeboxing.

━━━━━━━━━━━━━━━━━━━━━━
━━━━━━━━━━━━━━━━━━━━━━

What is a Product Owner's favourite Bond movie?

Re-View To A Kill.

Why don't Extreme Programmers eat apples?

Because they only do pear programming.

I just did a training course on writing amusing agile sermons.

I'm now a Certified Fun-Pastor.

What's brown and smells of
the Product Owner?

The Scrum Master's nose.

What do you call a business partner
who would give their right arm for
the product?

A Product Donor.

Why is Frozen a kanban coach's favourite film?

Because they let it F-L-O-O-O-W.

Why did the stupid ScrumMaster empty all the bins every day?

She was told she needed to eliminate waste.

What is a Product Owner's favourite Bond villain?

Dr No.

B.D.D. (*acronym*)

(1) Bullshit Driven Development.

The practice of trying to code something based on whatever crap comes out of the Product Owner's mouth today, only to have to completely re-write it the next day once they change their mind, sober up, get feedback etc.

(2) Behaviour Driven Development.

Something to do with gherkins and cucumbers that developers agree not to talk about outside of their cubicles.

Why did the stupid ScrumMaster delete the product backlog?

To maximise the amount of work not done.

**The Empowered
Product Owner**

**by
N. Igma**

Did you know, it's not actually "Agile"
unless it comes from the Agilé
region of France?

Otherwise, it's just a sparkling framework.

Why did the stupid ScrumMaster
rob a bank?

To pay off the team's technical debt.

A bad product owner from Trieste,
In their backlog was told to INVEST,
Things were so unrefined,
They got way way behind,
When they'll finish is anyone's guess.

My boss told me to go on Kanban training, so I looked it up on Wikipedia.

It said "Minimize work in progress."

So I didn't turn up.

Impediment (*noun*)

(1) A risk, issue, blocker, anything that means the development team can't get on with their work;

(2) The person who drags the team down;

(3) Management.

What do you get if you bring
three agile coaches into a room?

Four versions of agile.

What's the difference between a Product Owner and a battery?

A battery has a positive side.

A great way to write user stories is to use **The Three C's**:

Card
Conversation
Confirmation

Add an agile coach and you get a fourth **C**.

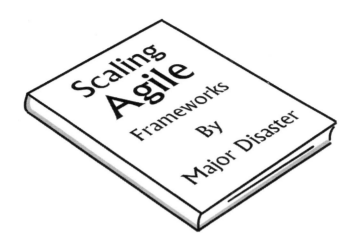

What's the difference between an agile coach and a trash can?

One's full of crap, the other is for waste disposal.

Mister T-Shaped (*noun, adjective*)

A generalising specialist who wears a lot of gold jewellery, drinks milk and doesn't get on planes.

What's the difference between an agile consultant and a flying pig?

The letter F.

Poxy Product Owner (*noun*)

Someone who claims to be a Product Owner but doesn't have the necessary time, authority or knowledge to do the job successfully.

Usually played by a business analyst.

Why did the stupid ScrumMaster
play planning poker with
his family?

Because he believed in
relative estimation.

Lean Six Sigma (*noun*)

Martial arts certification program for "agile
project managers". High achievers are able
to expose more pressure-points in agile teams
through the excessive use of useless metrics.

Why did the agile leader go to the chiropodist?

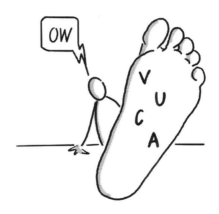

To treat their VUCA.

Continuous
Delivery

by
D. Ploy de Code

Why did the Product Owner run out of the planning session to the bathroom?

To work out their number two priority.

What do you call a business partner with a phobia of whales?

A Product Jonah.

I played planning strip poker
with the team today.

I thought mine was a Large,
but it turned out to be an
Extra Small.

Did you hear about the new type of
iterative, incremental and emergent
tagliatelle?

It's called Certified Scrum-Pasta.

A.T.D.D. (*acronym*)

Almost Test Driven Development.

Engineering practice where unit tests are written on post-its rather than into the codebase.

Did you hear about the failed entrepreneur who set up a commercial waterfowl racing league?

He was a terrible Pro-Duck Owner.

———————————————

Why did the stupid Scrum Master buy everybody an exercise bike?

Because she was told they were going lean!

Why can't you trust agile development team estimates?

Because they are all fib-onaccis.

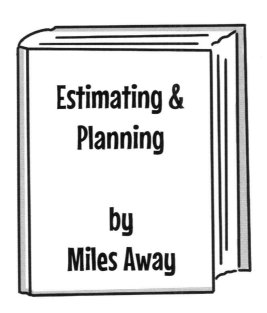

Estimating &
Planning

by
Miles Away

What do you call a business partner
who tells bad jokes?

A product groaner.

Have you heard about the
new pizza restaurant called
Fibonacci's?

They serve 5,8,13 or 21
slice pizzas.

Planning poker was so good we decided to try planning blackjack...

...but everything ended up being 21 points.

How many people do you think are in the #NoEstimates club?

No idea...nobody has ever tried to work it out!

What is JIRA useful for?

No...seriously...

What is JIRA useful for?

Why did the Scrum team hire the Pink Panther?

**Because he liked to get things
DONE-DONE...DONE-DONE...DONE-DONE DONE-DONE
DONE-DONE DONE-DONE DONE-DOOOOOOONE**

Getting Started With
Product Ownership

by
Ivor Backlog

I told my boss to go on an agile training course.

He told me his principles were already flexible enough.

My team told me to
"go get certified".

The diagnosis was OK, but the
jacket's a bit tight....

Did you hear about the ScrumMaster who was so devoted to timeboxing that they picked a fight with a grandfather clock?

Burnout Chart (*noun*)

A secret visualisation metric tracking the degree to which the team are "putting a shift in" to meet unrealistic demands and, as a result, creating technical debt.

Closely related to a dose of "JFDI".

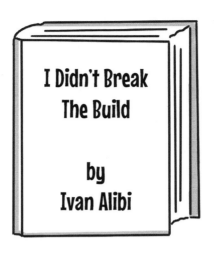

I Didn't Break
The Build

by
Ivan Alibi

I turned up to the sprint review
and a six foot beetle punched
me in the face.

Apparently there's a nasty bug
in the product.

Why does agile have such incorrect names?

SAFe isn't safe.
Extreme Programming is incredibly careful.
And Scrum doesn't let you punch someone in
the face behind the referee's back.

Much.

I'm not sure if we're doing SAFe wrong but the only PI that I've ever liked is Magnum.

Why would Santa Claus make a good
Scrum Master?

Because he is a fan of
elf-organising teams.

"Doctor, doctor...I've got a pain in the ass."

"How long have you had it?"

"He joined the team two weeks ago."

There are two types of Product Owner.

Those that prioritise the work and those that order...

...the team to do it.

My ScrumMaster introduced us to Magic Estimation today.

I dig the top hat but I'm not sure what we'll do with all the rabbits.

A sprint is a lot like making love...

You put a date in the diary.

You agree what you're going to do and how you're going to do it.

You get off to a fast start then try to last by working at a sustainable pace.

You check in regularly, aiming for mutual benefit.

Before finally discussing why it didn't go so well and whose fault it was.

Our Product Owner has
started writing our user
stories in braille.

Something weird is going on.
I can feel it.

I just did a training course to help me eliminate the uncomfortable pauses in my presentations.

I'm now a Certified Um-Master.

There are 10 types of developer in this world.

Those who love binary and those who don't.

There are two types of Kanbanner in the world, those that limit their WIP to 1 and...

Why do they call them estimates?

They're no friends of mine.

A young product owner from Belfast,
Asked his new agile team to forecast.
They were NoEstimate fans,
So messed up their sprint plan,
But at least they had managed to fail fast.

Bullshit Bingo:
Impress Your
Colleagues With Jargon

by
A. Giles-Crumb

Did you hear about the
agile coach who only
communicated through JIRA?

They were using
socraticket questioning.

I still believe in co-located teams.

We now co-locate our misery on to a Zoom call!

If the Product Owner is the voice of the customer, why does our customer sound like Darth Vader?

My Scrum project was so bad, the user stories were "Groundhog Day", "Titanic" and "Apocalypse Now".

Why did the agile coach refuse to use email?

Because he wanted to post-it.

MOB PROGRAMMING IN THREE WORDS:

MISERY LOVES COMPANY

MOST AGILE COACHES
COULDN'T EVEN SPELL
EXSTREEM PROGRAMING
LET ALONE TEACH IT.

I only invite pigs to
my standup.

But they make an
awful mess.

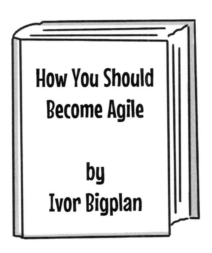

How You Should
Become Agile

by
Ivor Bigplan

I'm not saying our boss didn't understand Scrum, but our product goal was:

"Do all your work or you're fired!"

YOUR SPRINT IS SO LONG,
IT BREAKS THE ADVICE IN THE
LATEST VERSION OF THE SCRUM GUIDE
DOCUMENT CREATED BY TWO OF THE
ORIGINATORS OF SCRUM BACK IN THE MID 1990'S,
BASED ON IDEAS FROM A VARIETY OF
OTHER SOURCES INCLUDING A
RESEARCH PAPER
FROM JAPAN.

Why did the stupid ScrumMaster take his laptop bungee jumping?

To get into Extreme Programming.

My wife asked if I was committed to our marriage.

I told her it was more of a forecast and we would reflect at the end of every week.

My ex-wife asked if I was going to pay alimony.

I told her ScrumMasters don't do budgeting.

My lawyer said I would go to jail if I don't pay the divorce agreement.

I said I would run two-week experiments in prison to see if it is empirically the right practice for me.

It turns out that prison is more waterfall.

WHAT DO YOU GET IF YOU
BREED A LEGUME WITH A
SWISS ARMY KNIFE?

CROSS-FUNCTIONAL BEANS.

I'm not saying we're
doing it wrong but it's less of a
code freeze and more of a
code ice-age.

When my Product
Owner said it was
"story time", I didn't
expect to have to sit on
his knee.

Collective Nouns

A framework of agile coaches.

A consensus of ScrumMasters.

An indecision of Product Owners.

A disagreement of stakeholders.

An array of developers.

An invoice of consultants.

A platform of Release Train Engineers.

A muda of lean consultants.

A script of testers.

A hassle of recruiters.

An index of database administrators.

Did you hear about the agile professor who created a new kind of university with minimum start-up costs?

He started with a lean campus.

Did you hear about the Wright brothers' early experiments in aviation?

They were minimum fly-able products.

I just read a great book on listening.

I can't wait to tell the team all about it tomorrow.

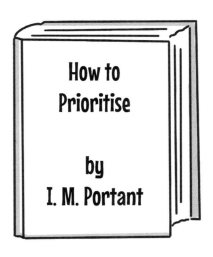

How to
Prioritise

by
I. M. Portant

Did you hear about the fanatical lean coach who was so devoted to minimising work in progress that they spoke a

L. E. T. T. E. R. A. T. A. T. I. M. E.

Our ScrumMaster said we had to hit our maximum velocity within 3 sprints.

But when we pushed him out of a plane he hit his maximum velocity in 12 seconds.

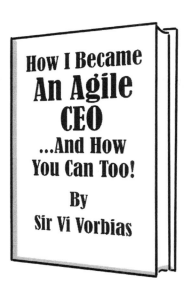

How I Became
An Agile
CEO
...And How
You Can Too!

By
Sir Vi Vorbias

I don't like calling my stakeholders chickens.

Stupid animals that squawk loudly, cluck constantly
and just shit on everything, should never be
compared to those fine birds.

I'm not saying my ScrumMaster doesn't like self-organisation, but she insists we call her "Your Majesty".

How many ScrumMasters does it take to change a lightbulb?

None.

It's not their job to do the work.

Fist of Five (*technique*)

(1) A facilitation tool to help teams reach consensus whereby each team member raises the number of fingers on one hand to indicate their level of support or agreement.

(2) Alternatively, a tool used by an "agile project manager" to help teams reach the RIGHT answer to "how long will this take?"...usually five punches is enough.

What's a Release Train Engineer's greatest fear?

A bus replacement service.

My last Kanban team's cycle time was so bad, it had more stages than the Tour de France.

Why did the stupid ScrumMaster buy 500 robots?

He wanted to do automated testing!

I just did a training course on marathon sprint finishes.

I'm now a
Certified Run-Past-Her.

As Sound as a Sutherland Stat (*simile*)

An outrageous claim that is quite blatantly too good to be true. Based on the sensationalist claims of Kiefer Sutherland when playing the character Jack Bauer in the TV show 24.

I went to a User Story workshop and asked the coach:

"How do you do User Stories?"

She said "You tell me."

"Sad news, as Charles George Sandersbuck failed today to become the first ScrumMaster to win the world meat-eating federation championship.

His tactical error was using agile principles in the final contest.

He finished the beef quickly, demolished the chicken in world record time but then he fell short at the last hurdle as he maximised the amount of pork not done."

A PO who lived near the Rhine,
Found herself in a really tough bind.
She found it so strange,
To be welcoming change,
But Scrum sure expanded her mind.

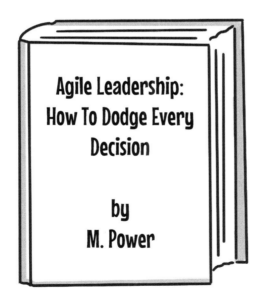

Agile Leadership:
How To Dodge Every
Decision

by
M. Power

Why are Product Owners bad at playing hide and seek?

Because it takes too long to agree on the definition of...

READY or not... here I come!!!

Scrum is like your Mother-in-law...

It will point out all of your faults, it won't help you out and you know that you'll never be good enough.

A young facilitator called Grace,
Was obsessed with using open space.
You could see from her face,
That her large marketplace,
Made her meetings a total disgrace.

WHAT DO YOU CALL A JEDI WHO HAS COMPLETED THEIR SCRUMMASTER TRAINING?

PEEBI-EYE KENOBI.

What's the difference between a ScrumMaster and hayfever?

One requires issues, and the other requires tissues.

Why was the Product Owner
refused a mortgage?

Because they already had too
much technical debt.

I just did a training course on
reporting on agile progress.

I'm now a Certified Board-Caster.

Why did the stupid
ScrumMaster make everyone
wear a traditional Turkish hat
to the retrospective?

Because he believed in fez-to-fez
communication!

Printed in Great Britain
by Amazon